Wash Day

BY Barbara H. Cole

ILLUSTRATED BY Ronald Himler

Star Bright Books

New York

Published in the United States of America by Star Bright Books, Inc., New York.
The name Star Bright Books and the Star Bright Books logo are registered
trademarks of Star Bright Books, Inc. Please visit www.starbrightbooks.com.

ISBN 1-932065-36-9

Printed in China
9 8 7 6 5 4 3 2 1

Library of Congress Cataloging-in-Publication Data

Cole, Barbara Hancock.
  Wash day / by Barbara H. Cole ; illustrated by Ronald Himler.
    p. cm.
  Summary: A young girl describes wash day, her favorite day of the
week, when Miss Ett the washerwoman comes with her grandson Sherman and
Grandpa tells stories and teaches Sherman to play music.
  ISBN 1-932065-36-9
  [1. Laundresses--Fiction. 2. Friendship--Fiction. 3.
Grandfathers--Fiction. 4. Music--Fiction.] I. Himler, Ronald, ill. II.
Title.
PZ7.C673413 Was 2004
[E]--dc22
                              2003021082

For Rena, Faith and Barbara's Red Hill guardian against
"ghoulies and ghosties, long leggitie beasties and things
that go bump in the night," with love — B.H.C.

For Andrea & Joe
     with love — R.H.

Miss Ett worked at most of the houses in the neighborhood, doing what people needed done. She helped some people weed gardens or rake leaves; she cleaned houses too, but she came to our house to wash clothes.

Mama dreamed about a washing machine, but they cost more money than we had. It was fine with me because of all the ordinary days (other than Christmas or school being out), wash day was the best of all. Miss Ett came early because the washing took most of the day, and she was better than any old washing machine.

She built her own fire around the wash pot. "I know what kind of fire I like," she said, "so I lay my own wood."

She filled the big black pot with water. As soon as it boiled, she dropped in the dirty clothes and pushed them under the bubbling water with a long stirring stick, worn smooth by many wash days.

"Get away from that fire," she ordered me and her grandson Sherman, who always came with her. "It's hot enough to burn you both up!"

That was Grandpa's cue to take over. "Come over here out of Ett's way," he said. "I have things to tell you." He was old and worn out, he said, but Sherman and I thought he was just right.

To keep us out of Miss Ett's way and the fire, he told us stories about being in the army when he was young and playing his trumpet all over the world. Sherman liked music better than anything, maybe as much as Grandpa. He was happy as a lark when Grandpa played the trumpet instead of talked about it.

He was even happier when Grandpa made him a reed flute and taught him to play *Taps*. "Sometimes when I played *Taps* in the army, the fog lay in the valleys in the early morning, and I'd blow so hard I'd blow that fog over the mountains, every wisp of it," he said.

Every wash day Grandpa played *Amazing Grace* because it was Miss Ett's favorite song. He'd drag the notes out long and slow, maybe to make it last longer. Miss Ett stopped her washing and leaned for a few minutes on the stirring stick, listening. When the song ended, she'd wipe her eyes on the corner of her apron and get back to her work.

"Once on Memorial Day, I played at the Tomb of the Unknown Soldier in Washington, D.C.," Grandpa told us. "The President and thousands and thousands of people came, and there was a flag on every grave.

That was a sight! The guards wore blue uniforms with shiny gold buttons and shoes with heeltaps that clicked when they turned to march in another direction. They looked like the tin soldiers I played with when I was a boy."

"Do you think *we* could march?" we asked Grandpa.

"Of course we can—with the right music," he said. And then he played *Yankee Doodle Dandy* while we marched right behind him around and around the wash pot and all around the back yard. Miss Ett laughed at us. "You three are a sight to behold, but I'd rather see you marching than playing in my fire." She rubbed the clothes on the scrub board, swinging and swaying to the music.

One wash day Sherman's eyes shone like new money. "Grandma Ett said I could get a trumpet for Christmas if she could work enough extra to pay for it," he said.

"Well, how about that!" Grandpa exclaimed. "In that case I'd better teach you another song," and they were at it again.

Yankee Doodle went to town riding on a pony; stuck a feather in his cap and called it macaroni. Yankee Doodle, keep it up; Yankee Doodle Dandy, mind your feather, mind your cap and with the girls be handy. The three of us marched. They played. I sang, and Miss Ett laughed. "You're a mighty quick learner," Grandpa said to Sherman, loving every minute as much as we did.

Sherman could play *Amazing Grace* on his reed flute by the time summer turned into cool nights and colored leaves and people were lighting fires to keep warm. Then something really sad happened. His family's house burned to the ground. The flute burned too. His Mama and Daddy went up North to get jobs, and he went to live with his Grandma Ett. Times were hard for them.

Not long after Sherman's house burned, Grandpa had a stroke and couldn't use his left arm. Wash day wasn't the same anymore. The music was gone.

Miss Ett kept washing our clothes, but she said they were harder to wash without the music. Sometimes Sherman and I marched around the yard, singing *Yankee Doodle*, but it wasn't the same without Grandpa and his trumpet.

It was time to start thinking about Christmas, but Sherman and I didn't talk much about that either. Nothing seemed right anymore.

Grandpa lay in bed all the time now. His trumpet in its worn case sat by his bedside like a silent, faithful friend. Sometimes he'd reach out and lay his right hand on it. I'd see his fingers move slowly, first one, then another, up and down, up and down. I imagined he was playing *Amazing Grace* in his head—the way Sherman and I could hear *Yankee Doodle* in our heads while we marched around and pretended things were like they used to be.

In the twilight on Christmas Eve, Grandpa called Mama to his room. She sat on the side of his bed and they talked a long time. Then she walked to Miss Ett's house to tell her Grandpa wanted to see her right away.

Miss Ett came and stood beside Grandpa's bed and held his hand. "I hope you're getting better," she said. "I really miss you on wash day."

"I feel good now," Grandpa said, "better than I have in weeks." And then he said, "Ett, I want you to take this trumpet to Sherman. There's a world of music left in it, and Sherman can play it out."

Miss Ett's eyes filled with tears.

"Tell Sherman to blow all the fog over the mountains, every wisp of it," Grandpa said. "He'll know what I mean."

Miss Ett laughed and squeezed his hand. "He'll make you proud," she said.

For Christmas I got the bicycle I had wanted for so long. In the early morning while the grass was still icy in the shadows, I rode all over the backyard and around and around the wash pot. Suddenly the air filled with one long blast that sounded as if it should have been music but wasn't quite.

Sherman!

All day he blew the trumpet, and gradually the sharp, choppy notes grew smooth. They drifted across the field and woods into our house right into Grandpa's bedroom. He smiled more that day than he had in weeks. By nightfall Sherman had played *Taps* so much I thought I could play it myself.

"What do you think, Papa?" Mama asked.

"That boy will blow the fog over the mountains before long. Just you wait and see. In a few more wash days he'll be playing *Amazing Grace*."

I fell asleep that night hoping Miss Ett would come wash tomorrow and before too long Grandpa and Sherman and I might march around the yard again.